Sniffy
The Beagle

By
Rita Eagle

Pictures by
G.B. Rasmussen

Sniffy the Beagle

Cover Image © Gerry Rasmussen
All right reserved. Used with permission.

Interior Images © Gerry Rasmussen
All right reserved. Used with permission.

Outskirts Press
http://www.outskirtspress.com

ISBN-10: 1-59800-537-5
ISBN-13: 978-1-59800-537-0

Outskirts Press and the "OP" logo are trademarks belonging to Outskirts Press, Inc.

Printed in the United States of America

For Adam and Emily

In loving memory
of Susan

Sniffy is a beagle hound.
He always has his nose to the ground.

Other dogs walk with their heads up high.
Sniffy's eyes never see the sky.

'Cause beagles like to sniff the ground.
That's what you do, if you are a hound.

Sniffy won't play with others, or fetch for a ball.
He won't play at frisbee; he won't PLAY at all !

He just stays by himself, nose close to the ground.
He has business to do, there is food to be found.

POPCORN

3

Sniffy was Tommy's dog but Tommy was sad.
Sniffy wasn't the dog Tommy wanted to have.

Tommy wanted a dog that held his head high,
A dog that caught frisbees from up in the sky.

He wanted a dog that would fetch and play,
Not a dog that kept sniffing and sniffing all day.

4

"I don't like my dog," Tommy told Mom one day.
"He makes me feel mad, 'cause he never will play.

"And I never asked for a sniffing hound,
And I don't want a dog with his nose to the ground.

5

"But you loved 'Sniff', said Mom, "when he was a pup.
Can't you love him a little, now that he's grown up?

He's just a little hound, you know,
Sniffing's what he's **meant** to do.

He's just a little beagle
Doing what he's got to do."

6

And Tommy sighed,
"Yeah... OK..., I guess."
('Cause he knew his mother
Usually knew best.)

But he still didn't want,
He had to confess,
A dog so different
From all of the rest.

7

Poor Sniffy! He **also** felt sad.
He didn't understand why Tommy was mad.

He loved little Tommy, and it made him feel bad
That Tommy didn't like the dog that he had.

Then, one morning, in the newspaper classifieds Tommy read an ad that would change both their lives!

The ad said:

WANTED:

" A sniffing hound.
One who KNOWS with his NOSE,
where food can be found.
We NEED such a dog to help us fight crime.
If you have such a dog, please call anytime,
for an interview with
Officer Sam Moriarity,
Chief Canine Trainer
at the Airport Authority."

10

Tommy was excited!!! He jumped up from his seat!
He HAD to do this! This really was neat!!

Sniffy's nose was amazing, Tommy had to admit,
You could **never** hide food. Sniffy'd **always** find it!!

"Heh Mom" he said, "Look at this!
P-L-E-A-S-E can we do it?
Can 'Sniff' go to the airport,
To be interviewed for it?"

The next day they were off, to the airport bound,
Tommy, Dad, and Mommy, and Sniffy the hound.

AIRPORT →

And Tommy was excited!
On this special day,

He hugged Sniffy tightly,
All of the way.

12

At the airport, the officer kindly explained
How Sniffy could help to keep **bad** things off planes.

"Dogs like Sniffy", he said, "can tell the police
If something that's bad is inside a valise.

And this they can do, 'cause they smell SO well,
They **smell** things that nobody else can smell.

In fact, they smell **four hundred** times better than us!
For smelling, your Sniffy's a real **Geni-us**".

13

GUNS   BOMBS   MEAT   PLANTS   FRUIT

NOT ALLOWED

ON PLANES

"But what ARE the bad things,"
Tommy asked Sam to tell,
"What are the **bad** things,
The dogs need to smell?"

"Guns and bombs," said Sam,
"Especially these.
But meat and plants too
And fruit from trees."

14

"Meat, plants and fruits!" Tommy exclaimed
"They do no harm!
Why keep **them** off the planes?"

"Cause they just might bring **germs**!
We have to inspect them!

So we need **special** dogs to help us detect them.
And the very best dog in the world for this,

The **very best 'detector'**
is a beagle, like Sniff."

15

Sniffy had been listening.
This job was a **dream**!

He wanted to be part
Of this canine team!

CANINE TEAM

16

So Tommy sent Sniffy to training school.

To learn the

FOUR DETECTOR RULES:

1. **Sniff** at the luggage; then if you smell
   Meat or a plant, it's your job to tell;

2. **Sit** by the suitcase, the one that you chose;

3. Put your **paw** on the suitcase, and

4. **Point** with your nose.

Sniffy sniffed, sat, and pointed, and put out his paw.
He loved his new job, upholding the law.

His uniform was green, and he wore it with pride.
"I'M WORKING" it said, in words on the side.

Then on one busy morning,
As Sniff did his job
Sniffing and pointing
For his handler Rob,

Sniffy saw something
That Rob did not see--
A suitcase being put
On a luggage dolly.

And though that suitcase
Had not been spied,
Sniffy could smell:
There was **meat** inside!!

21

The dolly moved fast —
It was soon out of the room!

Sniffy had to do something! —
There was no time to lose!

So as hard as he could,
He pulled on his leash.

And he pulled and he pulled
'Til his leash was released!

Then all through the airport, Sniffy did race

Until he caught up with that smelly suitcase!

The man who ran the conveyor belt
Was loading the bag
That Sniffy had smelled.

24

And he was going **INSIDE IT**!

26

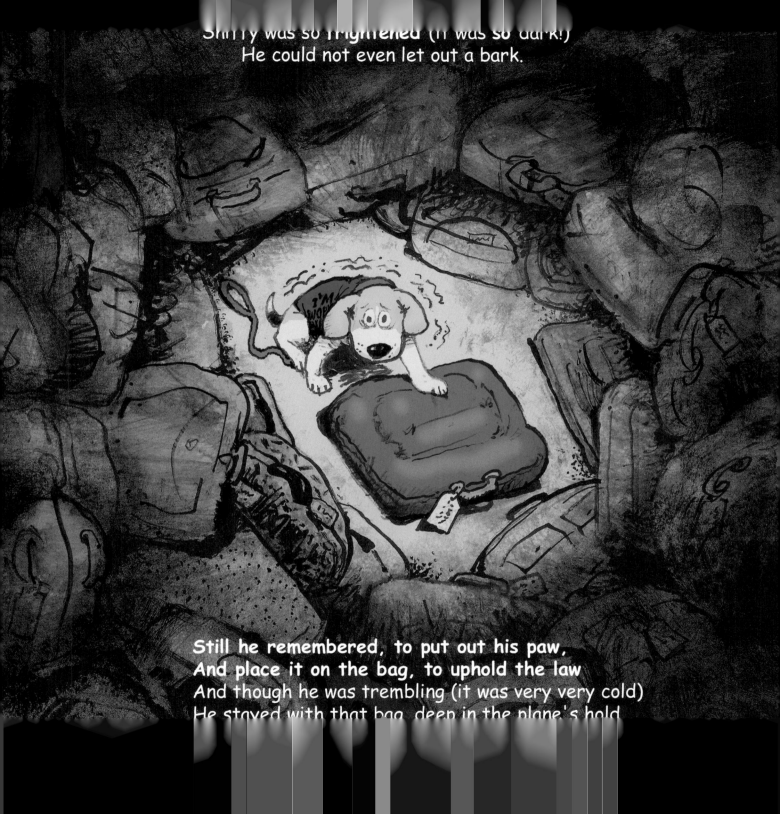

Shirty was so **frightened** (it was so dark!)
He could not even let out a bark.

Still he remembered, to put out his paw,
And place it on the bag, to uphold the law
And though he was trembling (it was very very cold)
He stayed with that bag, deep in the plane's hold

Until the plane landed,
And the luggage, released

To the passengers waiting...
And the Airport Police!

AND WHAT A SIGHT THEY THEN SAW!

Confused and exhausted, his uniform in rags,
A brave little beagle, sat amidst all the bags!

And everyone **cheered**, the moment they saw,
He was guarding the bag,
With an outstretched paw.

The police took the bag,
Then arrested the man
Who was bringing bad meat,
Into this land.

31

Then they sent Sniffy home, in a first class seat
With a warm drink, and a blanket, and good food to eat.

Then before family and friends, the Chief Airport Inspector
Gave Sniffy a medal, for "BEST EVER DETECTOR."

And Sniffy knew, when he heard the applause:
He was a hero for being... **just who he was.**

The moral of this story is clear,
There's something in each of us, to be held dear.
We are all God's children, and according to the plan,
There's **something** special in every man,
And woman, and child, and animal too.
There is something of value in each of you.

36

From Sniffy, Tommy learned a lot:
It's what you ARE that really counts,
And not, what you're NOT.